D0532174

For Amy Rennert.
Thank you for believing in me.
—P.R.

To Amy K.R.
—B.B.

In almost every way, it was an ordinary day in the Real World (but not *that* ordinary). Uni, the only unicorn who believed that little girls were REAL, was visiting.

How could this be true?

Well, Uni's friend, a strong smart wonderful magical little girl, had made the same wish as Uni at the exact same time. The clouds parted, the golden sun shone brightly, and a double rainbow appeared—the magic bridge between Here and There.

The little girl couldn't wait for Uni to meet her family and friends.

But when she introduced Uni to her parents,
they looked puzzled and just shook their heads.

The little girl was so disappointed!

Never mind, she thought. She knew her friends would love Uni as much as she did.

And the two raced to the park to meet them.

Along the way, they stopped to rescue a stray cat.

They played on the slide and took turns on the swings.

And they laughed and talked all afternoon while waiting for the little girl's friends to arrive.

When they did arrive and she introduced Uni to her friends, they looked confused.

Who was she talking about?

The little girl's friends laughed and said, "Ha, ha, ha, silly girl. Everyone knows unicorns don't exist! They're just make-believe."

Uni's magnificent mane drooped, and the magical horn brushed the ground.

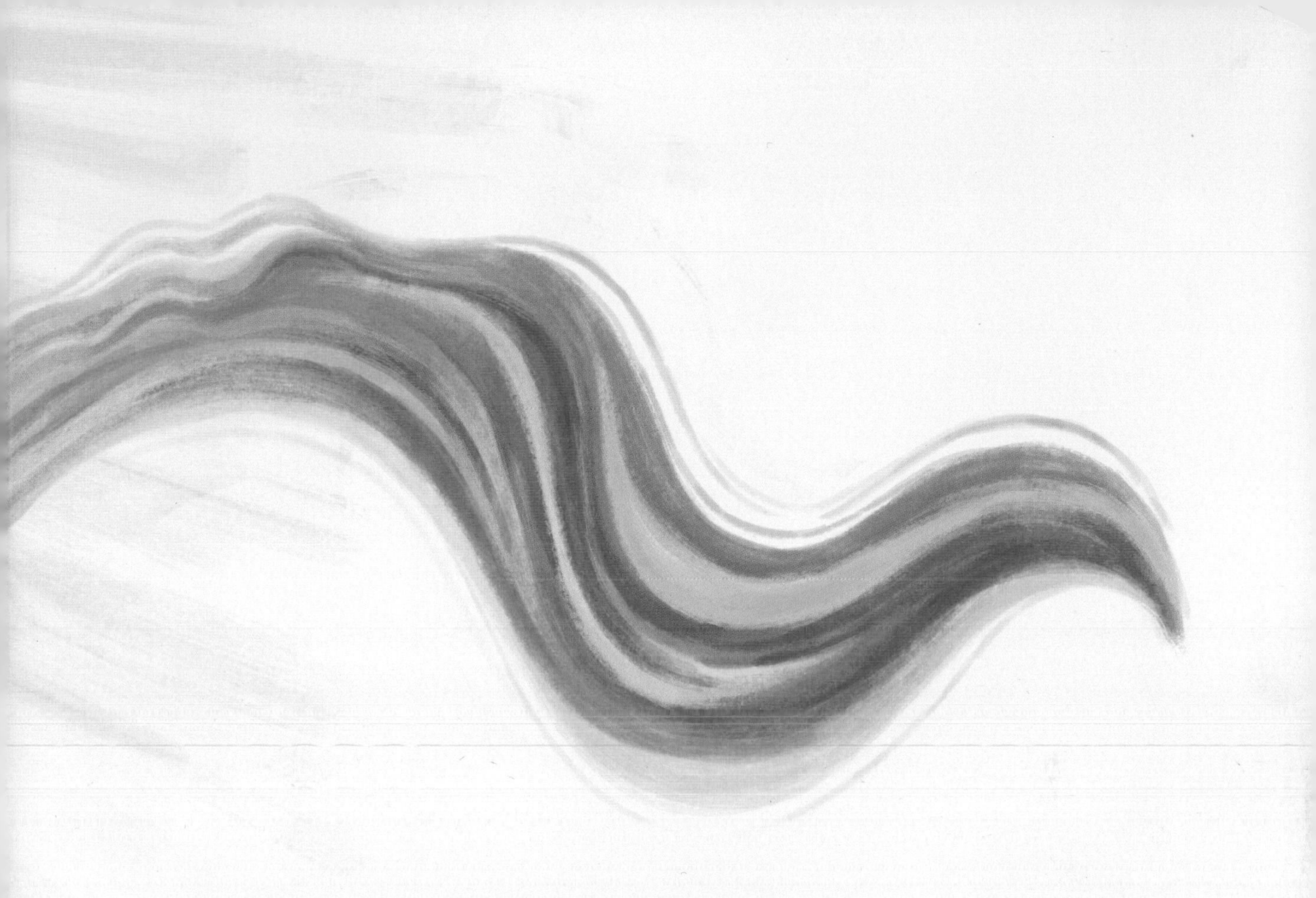

Just then, a ray of sunshine hit Uni's horn. There was a flash . . . and a rainbow appeared!

One little boy named Toby saw the rainbow and thought, Could it be?

"I see something!" he shouted. And as he became open to the sparkle of believing, he saw that unicorns did exist! They were really REAL.

The little girl smiled because she had never once doubted.